Big Sis Visits ~~~~

Written by Dr. Terri Major-Kincade

Illustrations by Mike Motz

This book is dedicated to all the siblings who wait for their baby brothers and sisters to come home from the NICU…
All the parents who wish their other children could visit their new baby brother or sister in the NICU and see more than just pictures and videos…

All the NICU doctors, nurses, social workers, respiratory therapists, occupational therapists, physical therapists, child life specialists, chaplains and volunteers who work so hard to make our NICU's family friendly.

This book is my dream for our NICU siblings. I hope one day it's a reality! Happy visiting.

Love,

Dr. Terri, aka ThePreemieDoc!

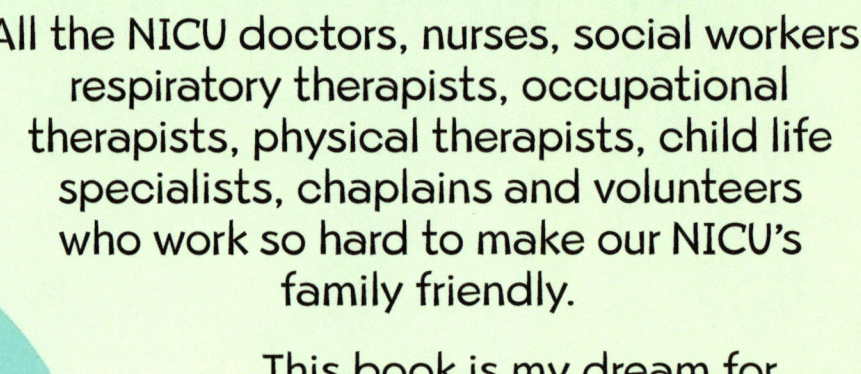

© 2021 Dr. Terri Major-Kincade. All Rights reserved.
No part of this publication may be reproduced or transmitted in any form or by any means, electronic, mechanical, including photocopy, recording, or any information storage and retrieval system, without permission in writing from the author.

I am going to be a big sister! I am so excited!
Mommy and I are getting everything ready for the baby's room!
We have clothes, toys, and diapers for my new baby brother.

Daddy is bringing home the baby crib today.
I am going to help him put it together.
Daddy says I am the best helper ever. I find piece one,
piece two, and piece three. They are almost as tall as me!

Mommy, Daddy, and I mark the day off the calendar every day.
It lets me know that in 6 weeks my baby brother will be on the way!

Daddy cooked my favorite breakfast today: pancakes, bacon, and eggs. I wonder if my baby brother will like this breakfast too, or will he want juice and fruit?

I eat my breakfast and run to the bus.
I see all my friends and wave to Mr. Gus.

Today at school is library day.
I ask for baby books from Ms. May.
I find books for my brother about
everything: dogs, cars, and even a King.

When I leave the library, my teacher has a note.
She says Daddy is coming early. We have a special place
to go and visit today.

I see my dad, and he tells me that my baby brother is coming today and that my mommy is with the doctor at the hospital!!

Daddy says my baby brother will be very small and will not be able to come home today at all.

We get to the hospital, and we find my mom.
She says, "Who is the best big sister ever?"
I say, "I am! Hi, Mom!"
She says "Hi! Your baby brother decided to come just a little early."
I hug my mommy really tight, and she shows me a picture
of my new baby brother.

The baby doctor comes to the room to tell my mommy and daddy how my baby brother is doing. Her name is Doctor Terri.
She shakes my hand and tells me that my baby brother can't wait to meet me. But first she wants to tell me about the ICU nursery!

The ICU Nursery, or NICU, is the place where babies go when they are born early. Sometimes they are very sick. I have to be very quiet in the nursery, and I can only visit if I am not sick, so my baby brother does not get sick.

I say, "Okay, Dr. Terri! I understand. Very quiet! Not Sick! Got it!"
Then she tells me when we get to the ICU Nursery, I have to wash my hands and that my brother will be in a plastic box called an incubator.

I am so excited!! I ask Dr. Terri if I can come now. She tells me I can. I am old enough to visit the ICU Nursery because I am 6 and have had all my shots! They have a special time for siblings to visit every day.

Sometimes, though, you must wait until your baby brother or sister can come home to see them, but you can still look at pictures and video that your mommy and daddy take for you.

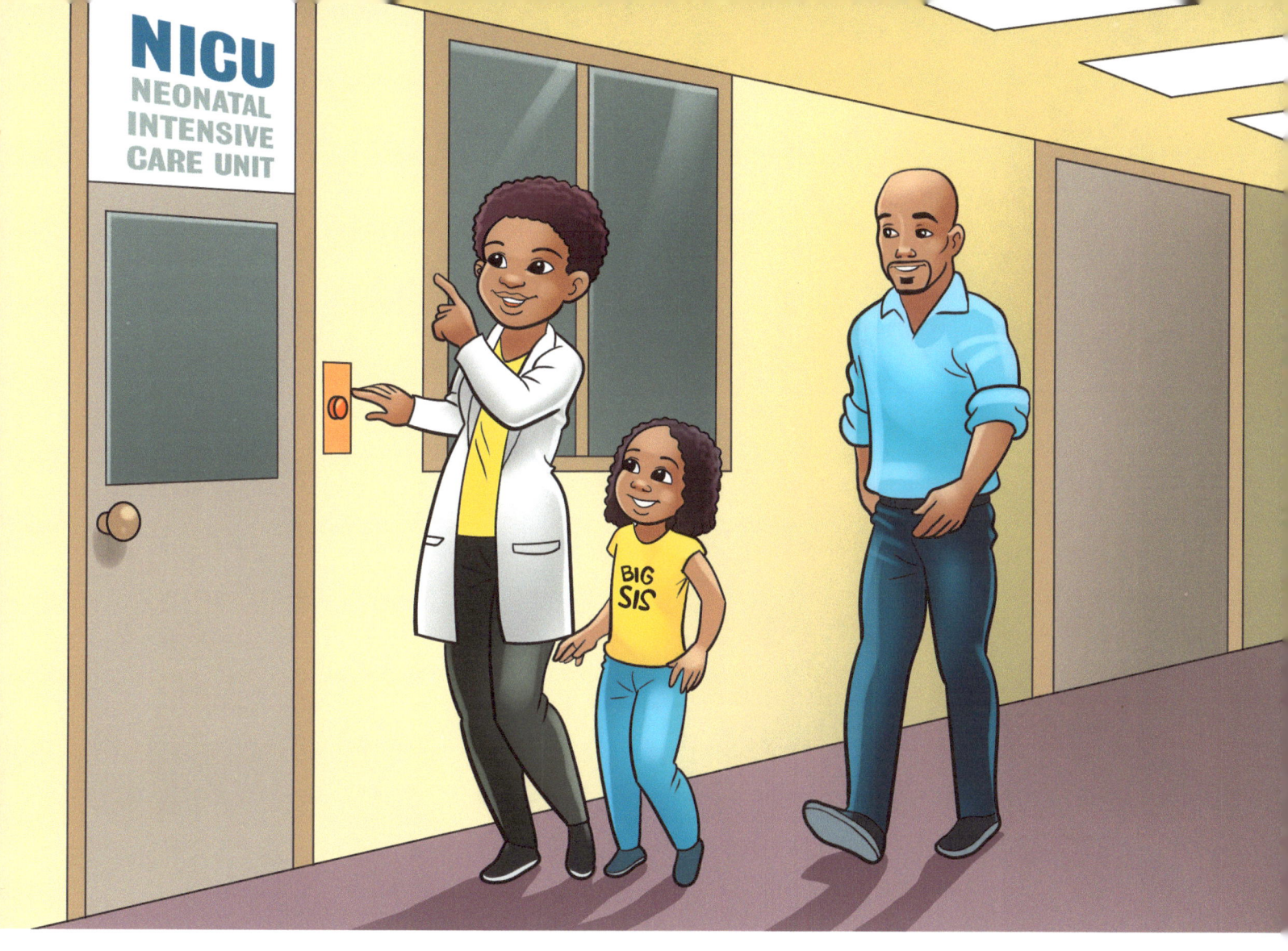

"Yaaay!!" I say. "Daddy, can we go now?"
He says, "Yes, Big Sister, we can!"
Mommy is going to take a nap. She tells me to have a good visit.
We follow Dr. Terri to the ICU Nursery. I see the letters N-I-C-U.
I ask Dr. Terri what it stands for. She says, "Neeee Ohhh Naaaatal
Innnn tensive Care Unit!" I think I will stick with NICU.

Dr. Terri presses a button, and the doors open.
I walk in holding Daddy's hand. We wash our hands at the sink.
Dr. Terri reminds us to sing Happy Birthday two times to make
sure we wash our hands for 20 seconds. Daddy sings first, then me!
Dr. Terri is smiling.

Now we follow Dr. Terri to my baby brother. I see lots and lots of plastic houses. Dr. Terri calls those incubators or isolette. When we get to my brother's bed, Dr. Terri introduces me to his nurse, Nurse Lynn. She is nice.

Nurse Lynn says, "Hi! What's your name?"
I say, "Hi, my name is Nicole. I'm the big sister, and that's my baby brother, Charlie!"
Nurse Lynn smiles and says, "It's very nice to meet you!"

Nurse Lynn takes the cover off the isolette,
and I finally see my baby brother. He is sleeping and has
some plastic tubing on his nose. Nurse Lynn says that is oxygen
to help him breathe. I watch his chest go up and down.

I do not see any clothes, but I do see his diaper.
I ask Dr. Terri if he is cold.
She says, "No, the incubator keeps him warm
just like incubators for eggs for baby chicks.
He has a shiny gold heart on his chest that tells the isolette
how to keep him warm." I laugh. My little brother
is staying warm like a baby chick.

Daddy asks if it is okay for me to touch his fingers and toes like he did when he came before me. Nurse Lynn says, "Did you wash your hands?"
I say, "Yes!"
She says, "Okay, let's do it!"

I slowly raise my hand, and Nurse Lynn guides my finger through the open doors on the isolette. They are called portholes, like the holes on a ship!
I say "Hi, baby brother! I am your big sister!" He grabs my finger, and I laugh. Daddy takes my picture for Mommy.

I ask Dr. Terri, "What is in my brother's nose?"
She says it is a special tube that goes from his nose to his stomach.
He will get milk through the tube in his nose until
he gets bigger, and his lungs are stronger.

I ask her if the tube hurts my brother. She says, "No it does not."
The tube is called a nasogastric tube or NGT for short.
Daddy says, "That's a really big word for a 6-year-old!"
We agree to tell Mommy it's an NG tube!

Dr Terri has stepped away from the bedside to see another baby. I ask Nurse Lynn what is in my brother's arm. It looks just like the tubing my mommy has. Nurse Lynn says it is a called an IV. It is a special tubing that goes from the skin to my brother's veins.

It gives him fluid and medicines to help him get better. The fluid looks like water to me, but Nurse Lynn says it's not water. It has sugar and something called electrolytes to make sure he gets everything he needs.

Dr. Terri has come back, and now Daddy and I are sitting on a rocker in the NICU, talking to Dr. Terri. I ask Dr. Terri how long my baby brother will be in the ICU Nursery. She says that since he was born six weeks early that he may be in the ICU Nursery for 4 to 6 weeks.

This makes me very sad. I don't want to leave him. Daddy hugs me and says that he and Mommy are sad too, but Charlie needs to get big and strong and this will give us time to get everything else ready for him. I say, "Okay, Daddy! That sounds like a good plan!"

Dr. Terri asks Daddy if he has any other questions, he says no and thanks Dr. Terri and Nurse Lynn for taking care of my brother. I say thank you too! I turn to my baby brother and say, "See you soon, Charlie!" Then I grab Daddy's hand and wave bye to Dr. Terri and Nurse Lynn. I can't wait to tell Mommy about our visit to the NICU.

We get back to Mommy's room, and she is sitting up in bed eating her dinner. She says, "Hi, Nicole. How is Charlie doing?"

I say, "Mommy, he is doing great. He was sleeping.
I learned all about the NICU. We washed our hands,
saw the isolette, and learned about oxygen and feeding tubes.
Charlie has an IV just like you!"
Mommy smiles. "You learned a lot! You are going
to be a great big sister."

I smile and look at Mommy and Daddy and say,
"Guess what was the best part?!"
Daddy says, "What?"
I say, "When Charlie grabbed my fingers!
He knows I am his big sister!"
Mommy and Daddy smile and say, "Yes! Yes, He does! Thanks for helping us to take care of him. He will be home before you know it."

I say, "Thanks, Mom... Now can I have some of your ice cream?"
She says, "Yes," but not before she dips her finger into
the ice cream and puts some on my nose!
Daddy laughs and so do I. I can't wait for Charlie
to have ice cream on his nose too!

Dr. Major-Kincade was first introduced to America over 20 years ago as the young Neonatologist featured on ABC's *Houston Medical* and Lifetime's *Women Docs*. She received her bachelor's degree from Prairie View A&M University and her Medical and Master's in Public Health's Degrees from UCLA. Dr. Terri completed her pediatric residency training at UT Southwestern Children's Medical Center of Dallas and her Perinatal-Neonatal Fellowship training at UT Houston Health Science Center, Memorial Herman Children's Hospital.

She is a highly requested keynote speaker, known in the industry for her authenticity and compassion in discussing challenging topics around racial health disparities, physician-patient communication, and neonatal palliative care. Her career in Neonatology was in inspired by her own sister, who was born three months early in 1968. Dr. Terri is a two-time best-selling author and has been featured in *Ebony*, NBC, Huggies, and BlackDoctor.org. She previously served as Chair for the Texas March of Dimes Steering Committee for African American Outreach and currently serves as the Chair for the Diversity, Equity Inclusion Committee for the National Board of Pregnancy Loss and Infant Death Alliance (PLIDA), The Clinical Advisory Board of The Return To Zero HOPE Foundation and is a new member of the Pampers Womb to World Advisory Board, where she provides expertise in addressing Maternal and Infant Health Disparities.

Dr. Terri, or Dr. Boo as she is affectionately called, defines her mission as a commitment to empower families to make informed choices for their babies at a time when they believe they have no choice, as well as to empower physicians and nurses to help families making those difficult choices. Dr. Terri has been happily married over 25 years and lives in Dallas, Texas, with her husband and two children.

For more information about Dr. Terri, booking opportunities, or book sales, please visit **drterrimd.com**.

CPSIA information can be obtained
at www.ICGtesting.com
Printed in the USA
LVHW071451280323
742831LV00019B/235